WITHDRAWN

POEMS *by Philip Schultz*

DEEP WITHIN THE RAVINE

VIKING

VIKING
Viking Penguin Inc., 40 West 23rd Street,
New York, New York 10010, U.S.A.
Penguin Books Ltd, Harmondsworth,
Middlesex, England
Penguin Books Australia Ltd, Ringwood,
Victoria, Australia
Penguin Books Canada Limited, 2801 John Street,
Markham, Ontario, Canada L3R 1B4
Penguin Books (N.Z.) Ltd, 182–190 Wairau Road,
Auckland 10, New Zealand

Copyright © Philip Schultz, 1980, 1981, 1982, 1983, 1984
All rights reserved

First published in 1984 by Viking Penguin Inc.
Published simultaneously in Canada

ISBN 0-670-26609-4
Library of Congress Catalog Card Number: 83-40641

With special gratitude to the Corporation of Yaddo and the MacDowell Colony, where many of these poems were written, and to the New York Council on the Arts (Creative Artists Public Service Program) and the American Academy and Institute of Arts and Letters, for awards which enabled me to work on this book.

Acknowledgment is made to the following periodicals in which some of the poems in this book appeared originally:

The American Poetry Review: " 'Deep Within the Ravine' "; *The Brockport Forum:* "I'm Not Complaining" and "My Smile"; *Choice:* "Balance"; *The Georgia Review:* "My Guardian Angel Stein"; *The Kenyon Review:* "Ode," "Mrs. Applebaum's Sunday Dance Class," "In Exile" (under the title "Dante In Exile"), "Shane," "Pumpernickel," "Interior with Arches: After Piranesi," "For My Mother," "Ode to Desire," and "Guide to the Perplexed"; *Michigan Quarterly Review:* "Personal History" and "The Ogre"; *The Nation:* "The Wish," "His Face," "Anemone," "Jerusalem," "The Quality," and "Approaching Forty"; *New Orleans Review:* "A Person"; *The New Yorker:* "The View"; *The North American Review:* "Late Night Phone Calls"; *Pequod:* "A Letter Found on a January Night in Front of the Public Theater"; *Poetry:* "Lines to a Jewish Cossack: For Isaac Babel" and "The Garden of Honor" (revised and retitled "Guide to the Perplexed").

"Ode" also appeared in *The Pushcart Prize, IV* (Best of the Small Presses), 1981–82 edition; "Mrs. Applebaum's Sunday Dance Class," "Pumpernickel," and "The View" appeared in *The Anthology of Magazine Verse & Yearbook of American Poetry,* 1981, 1983, and 1984, respectively.

Page 67 constitutes an extension of this copyright page.

Printed in the United States of America
by R. R. Donnelley & Sons Company, Harrisonburg, Virginia
Set in Garamond
Designed by Roger Lax

For Sylvia & Zane Liff

He sang
and fourteen hundred years
later, it reappears—
    in the barrel's bung . . .
codex from wine-bung springing,
as from the dung
    —the rose.

CATULLUS

DEEP WITHIN THE RAVINE is the 1984 Lamont Poetry Selection of The Academy of American Poets.

From 1954 through 1974 the Lamont Poetry Selection supported the publication and distribution of twenty first books of poems. Since 1975 this distinguished award has been given for an American poet's second book.

Judges for 1984: Louise Gluck, Charles Simic, and David Wagoner.

Contents

Ode to Desire

Ode to Desire

Remember how we watched a hang-glider lift himself
between heaven & earth & the music in the sway
of his arms & how for a moment he was one with the light
& as perfect as the world allows—as if love were a kind
of weather where one moment there is a calm so complete
the earth rolls on its side like a woman turning
in the generous folds of her sleep & then thunder
strikes like the despair of total embrace?

Remember the newsreels of marathon dancers,
how they cling like shadows long after the music
of first passion, how they push & drag each other
like swimmers stretching toward the surface light
of their desire to continue the embrace
another quarter turn round the speckled floor?

To think that after we have given up all hope
of perfection I am still jealous of the red towel
you wrap round your raisin hair & of the photos
of you as a child who looked happy enough not to know me
& that I still cannot understand the blood's rush to give all
& the urgency that opens in my chest like an umbrella
which will not close until you take me back
into the tides of your breath!

What rage, our bodies twisted like wires
in the brain's switchboard, hurt plugged to joy,
need to desire, how it happens so quickly, this entering
of another's soul, like molecules of fire connecting
flesh & dream in the sheets of a hundred beds, spring
suddenly knocking at the window as your long female body
sprawls into full radiance, ah, such high laughter
in light-flushed rooms, our bodies so perfectly crossed!

Remember the night we read how the female whale whips
her tail out of reach as the male splits the ocean
plunging round her for whole days & nights crying
such symphony of rage birds whirl round their spindrift waltz
as the sea is shaken like a fishbowl & the sky is shredded
into ribbons of light? Yes, it is curious, the risk of such
attraction, but isn't there implanted in the anemones of her eyes
the smallest smile?—for all creatures large & small must realize
that in stirring such passion the prize must be worth the promise
& yes, I am tired of this endless dancing in circles & suddenly
the light of this spring morning does not throw back its color
so splendidly as before though there is still the joy that comes
only after long pain as you slip slowly within reach & everywhere
the air burns like the stained glass in the attic window
where I sat as a boy listening to the wind with such longing
the light itself was song!

The View

Remember how the door in our first apartment always stuck?
Now the building is a Chinese laundry & the Spaniard,
who kept us up clapping flamenco, asked where you were.

I admitted I didn't know. Perhaps too much happens
& the loss is finally for something that never existed?
Returning may be a step forward, but now the question

is how much we can bear to question. Change, I think,
happens almost always too late. Yes, I still miss
the way you washed your hands before undressing & how

your green eyes darkened with desire. I remember
what was promised. That once I believed I could die of love.
That, like fate & youth & weather, it continued forever.

This is the first day of the new year & around me everywhere
the light is less convincing. I mean to say the view this morning
from every direction is still lovely, if a little darker.

To a Young Woman of Ambition

It is a shame we cannot keep the brilliance
of this dreaming that burns the flesh like sunlight,
but remember how at first I protested the difference

in our age & you laughed that time does not make a man
less fearful? Yes, I feared the joy of your passion
which blossomed with such invention I was more admirer

than teacher. But now you say there is no solace
& must choose between love & ambition as if the heart
is a prism in which each pleasure must be fractured.

Now you are dizzy from this spinning & I wish I could
replace our first excitement but desire is a moment
in which we constantly awaken to the mystery of our nature,

a gift, like first speaking, in which the words do not obey,
but make their own fine music. I think the choice is the risk
of merging with another, not jeopardy or damage, but permission

to know the body's grammar, which is a kind of singing.
Like children waking in the heat of dreaming, perhaps
we cannot live long in this light, but think of how

our flesh has been sweetened & of the lovely story
we have made of nothing. It is now yours to sing
like a poem that cannot live another moment without expression.

I'm Not Complaining

It isn't as if I never enjoyed good wine
or walked along the Hudson in moonlight,
I have poignant friends & a decent job,
I read good books even if they're about
miserable people but who's perfectly happy,
I didn't go hungry as a kid & I'm not constantly
oppressed by fascists, what if my apartment
never recovered from its ferocious beating,
no one ever said city life was easy, I admit
my hands turn to cardboard during love-making
& I often sweat through two wool blankets—
but anxiety is good for weight-loss, listen,
who isn't frightened of late night humming
in the walls, I don't live in a police state,
I own a passport & can travel even if I can't
afford to, almost everyone is insulted daily,
what if love is a sentence to hard labor &
last year I couldn't pay my taxes, I didn't
go to prison, yes, I've lost friends to alcohol
& cancer but life is an adventure & I enjoy
meeting new people, sure it's hard getting older
& mysteriously shorter but insomnia & depression
afflict even the rich & famous, okay, my folks
were stingy with affection & my pets didn't live long,
believe me, sympathy isn't what I'm after, I'm basically
almost happy, God in all His wisdom knows that at heart
I'm really not complaining . . .

Mrs. Applebaum's Sunday Dance Class

Her red pump tapping, ankle-length gown slit at the knee,
Mrs. Applebaum lined us up as her husband tuned his piano,
his bald head shining under the Temple's big bay windows.
I can see it all again, the girls' shy smiles, the boys' faces
scrubbed bright as strawberries, 200 fingers anticipating trouble,
the bowing & curtsying rehearsed to a nervous perfection
by Mrs. Applebaum's high German class—it isn't hard to envision
Sarah Rosen, her bourbon curls tied in a ponytail, stepping forward
like an infant swan to choose that clod Charlie Krieger,
while smiling at me! Call it first intimation of splendor,
or darker knowledge, but can't you see us, twenty dwarfs
colliding Sunday after Sunday, until, miraculously, a flourish here,
a pivot there, suddenly Davie Stern dipping Suzie Fein
to Mrs. Applebaum's shrill, "Und vonce agunn, voys und gurdles!"

Oh Mrs. Applebaum, who could've guessed our wild shoving
would be the start of so much furor? You must've known
there was more to come when our lavish stretching left us dizzy,
clumsy with desire? Weren't you, our first teacher, thinking
of the day when such passion would finally take our teeth & hair?
What really channeled such light into your eyes & swayed
your powerful bosom with such force? What pushed Mr. Applebaum,
never a prize winner, to such heights? Ah Mrs. Applebaum,
didn't you notice how I sighed when Sarah didn't change partners
& stayed in my arms? I'm speaking of that terrible excess,
not the edging back, but the overflowing of all that color
flowering in our cheeks! Please, Mrs. Applebaum, remember
Sarah in pink chiffon foxtrotting, her head back & braced teeth
pressed against all that which was to come—the world of such
profound promise! Yes, remember Sarah, her eyes, for so few moments,
so blue the room everywhere around us filled with light!

My Smile

My smile won my mother trips to Niagara Falls
three years running, my black-eyed I'll-eat-
the-world-for-you twinkle of unabashed lechery
beat out every other five-year-old in Rochester, N.Y.
In one photo I'm folded artfully on a counter, my arms
twisted over my suspendered little chest like straps
in a straightjacket from which I'm struggling to burst free
like a pintsized Houdini. The suspenders alone are a stroke
of genius. My mother understood the appeal of a small boy
eager to please the female world with a wistful imitation
of masculine bravura. She knew the dark light in my eyes
came straight from the reptilian brain which owns only
one instinct: delight. Her point was appetite. You see,
I was her second chance to dazzle the world with a fire
unlike anyone else's so she fanned mine with stories
of Attila the Hun & Madame Bovary & warned me against
hiding inside bells like Quasimodo whose shyness
was uglier than his face. She herself wanted to burst open
like a poppy seed but was too frightened to reveal her brilliance.
Believe me, neither of us had much choice. My smile became
a fossil souvenir of her own desire which Quasimodo would understand.
His smile also meant business. Listen, I could go on forever about this
& with any luck, I will.

Pumpernickel

Monday mornings Grandma rose an hour early to make rye,
onion & challah, but it was pumpernickel she broke her hands for,
pumpernickel that demanded cornmeal, ripe caraway, mashed potatoes
& several Old Testament stories about patience & fortitude & for
which she cursed in five languages if it didn't pop out fat
as an apple-cheeked peasant bride. But bread, after all,
is only bread & who has time to fuss all day & end up
with a dead heart if it flops? Why bother? I'll tell you why.
For the moment when the steam curls off the black crust like a strip
of pure sunlight & the hard oily flesh breaks open like a poem
pulling out of its own stubborn complexity a single glistening truth
& who can help but wonder at the mystery of the human heart when you
hold a slice up to the light in all its absurd splendor & I tell you
we must risk everything for the raw recipe of our passion.

Counterparts

Late at night my stillborn sister lives in me
like an unspent spirit, deep in that dark
from which I too come, each of us forever
expatriate & incomplete like a face split
by light & shadow. I mean deep in the nucleus
of our being there is a harmony of instinct
that is neither male nor female but a quality
of strength in which we fuse like the four islands
of the infant skull which fit so perfectly her eyes
open inside mine to that spray of worldly light
that stuns only the living. I mean a bonding
so electric the fugue of our otherness makes
a music so fine we spin within each other's gravity
like earth & sky from dark to light until mind & flesh
embrace & I understand at last why all love must be
incestuous.

For My Mother

The hand of peace you sent from Israel
hangs on my wall like an ironic testament
to the one quality we have never shared.
I imagine you peering into that ancient vista
as if discovering God in the brilliant sunlight,
worrying no doubt about your bunions & weak ankles.
These words have been a long time in coming.
Once I wrote only to the dead but grief has an end.
The living are more demanding. I have seen the scar
big as a zipper on your belly where they cut you open
& ripped out six pounds of hunger demanding to be adored.
You named me Big Mouth, Big Pain, Big Wanting. Sons,
you said, suck a woman dry & leave for someone
with stronger ankles & a back better suited
to their talent for self-eulogy. Yes, men
are more selfish. Nothing demands of us
so absolute a generosity. But I have given up
the umbilicus of rage which for so long has fed me.
Now I understand why you paste every scrap of my existence
in a black book like a certificate of blood, but achievement
is not redemption & even now I cannot hold a woman
without fearing she might take too much of me. Perhaps
this is why I love a woman most during her time
when the earth is lush within her & her embrace
gives forth such privilege my passion for distance
becomes a cry for forgiveness, a desire to return
always to the beginning. No, I have not forgotten
the Saturday afternoons in movie houses when you
cried so softly I imagined I was to blame.
I remember those long walks home,
our hands a binding of such unbreakable vengeance
I can still taste the cool blue wafers of your eyes.

Believe me, there was nothing I would not have given,
nothing I would not have done for you. Remember our game
when I held your leg so tightly you had to drag me
like a ball & chain around our unhappy house? Neither of us
understood that the grip of consanguinity is nothing less
than an embrace with time. Mother, though I cannot unhinge
all this lasting sorrow or make your flesh sing, cannot
return the gift of such remarkable expansion, I am always
thinking: This is for you, this word, this breath, this tiny light,
this, my hand of peace, this wound which does not heal.

The Wish

The Wish

The mind is a plant
stuck in dark heavy water

each night it opens
demanding friends books

affectionate reassurance
yet it remembers every failure

imperfection please I whisper
into the wound of its ear

forgive the lives wasted
the shame digested & wake

from this history of fear
this dross of consanguinity

which breaks like surf
in the arms of loved ones

where night after night
I wade through the mud

of inherited nightmare
looking for the end of longing

the grease of sunlight yes
there is always the wish

for regeneration the wish
to fit this world of dark

abstraction where I wander
like a sleepwalker dreaming

the story of his life
in a coma of cold rooms

His Face

Once he wished
to wear his face
quietly as a shadow,
now it startles him
with its tics which
seem less cautious
while the light deep
in his eyes seems more
familiar in its strangeness.
Now his hair has revolted
& the weight in his cheeks
is impacted with, what—
desire? His body is never
this much trouble. Something
is still missing or wrong
around his eyes when he
sees himself suddenly
in shop windows, as if
his expression did not
fit his feelings. I think
something remains stuck
in him, some stubborn light
that stays damaged despite
each year's new mortgage
of spirit. Call it what
you like, yet somehow
his face survives its
wealth of hours, while
his smile holds back
its hurt as the life
behind it keeps ebbing,
if fitfully, like laughter
in an empty bed.

Late Night Phone Calls

All night the man upstairs walks to Madam Butterfly,
dragging his body like something he must be rid of,

every night this human scraping at the stillness
as you stare into the window light across the courtyard

as if it were a kind of truth,
a preoccupation with the significance of details

like the shrill human cry
three buildings away

which isn't ecstasy or pride
but a fact in the ongoing mystery of our lives,

such as when the phone rings just before dawn
& no one speaks & the hush at the far end

splits the last shred of darkness
into a tuning fork of light & everything you fear

or desire is known by a stranger
who means you the greatest harm

& you watch the dark curl off the roofs
lifting yourself like a swimmer out of one dream into another,

grasping at the phosphorescent surface of the world
which, like the light across the courtyard,

no one ever turns off,
not all night long.

Balance

Eight years gone & the welfare building is a parking ramp.
The attendant can't recall where it went. Uptown somewhere, he thinks.
But ten thousand people filled those halls & only the ocean
is a carpet big enough to sweep so many under.

I was a clerk who read Chekhov & knew the fate of clerks.
I learned to sway down halls like a dancer & never stop to listen.
Mornings I filed dental reports & wore earplugs against the crying
for crutches, steel hands & mattresses fitted to broken backs.

A Mrs. Montvale perched on my desk & swore she'd kill herself
if her new dentures didn't arrive by Thanksgiving.
A fatalist with rotting gums, she feared dying toothless at a feast.
Near closing time the ghosts lined up around the block, still waiting.

In Central Index I watched the hundred Ferris wheels
flip rainbow cards sorting the dead from the quickly dying
& filed the electric buzz of computers into a symphony so grand
it washed the curdled voices from my head.

I'm glad the building's gone. Despair can't be tolerated
in such numbers & Gray's *Anatomy* doesn't explain
how the human body breaks a hundred ways each day & still finds balance.
Lord of Mercy, the dead still need bus fare & salvation!

Guide to the Perplexed

Maimonides believed despair was a luxury
of good intentions gone bad & that nobody
had it worse than 12th-century Jews who
married their misery & sired whole tribes
of woe-ridden supplicants but I wonder
if he ever received mail asking him to
reserve burial space in a veterans' cemetery
when his 4-F during the last war was a
matter of record or if the Committee for
an Extended Lifespan demanded he know why
others outlived him by at least 30 years
(did he smoke, drink, eat raw flesh or
engage in deviant sexual-religious practices?)
or if his Congressman harassed him to support
a bill against abortion, implying he murdered
his own kind or if his dreams replayed nightly
a pornographic commedia dell'arte in which
his woman left him for someone who sold
penis enlargers to aging bureaucrats or if
strangers called at all hours insisting
his number was listed in the S&M Newsletter
& if he was invited annually to a benefit
sponsoring the World's End—yes, he believed
in forced recognitions & diplomacy (doctoring
his enemies, he buttered both sides of every
psyche) but even Spinoza found him perplexing
(in fairness Spinoza found everyone confusing)
& often a faith's best defender is also its
worst enemy but what good really is his
fancy system for spiritual ecstasy when death
comes early in dishonorable graves while a
generation of unborn souls curse our memory
in cataracts of junk mail—did he ever weary
of Nature's magic show & desire only to lie
on his brown couch, sighing so profoundly

each rib snapped like a violin string—ah,
Maimonides, I know the 20th century is through
(friends call to remind me) & the latest history
of our time is entitled: *Vanity, Greed, Intolerance
& 30 Days to Thinner Thighs,* but am I responsible
for every abomination east of the China Sea—
Vietnam wasn't my fault & I'm not capable of
inflating the National Deficit!—Rabbi,
I realize 6,000 years of impacted grief & guilt
cannot be deducted from our taxes, but the real
question remains: what happened between your time
& mine that delivered us into the hands of
modern Manhattan?

The Ogre

He is small,
awkward & his left eye

floats as if pulled
in the wake of a cloud.

Once I wept to watch him
with other children. He

could not understand
that their rejection

was not meant to destroy him.
Such ugliness is a blessing

he must live against, I think.
Like the world's opaque beauty,

it is a gift
which will possess him.

Yes,
like a father's love,

his imperfection
will sustain him.

A Person

gets so tired like I was telling
my daughter Kate have you ever
pulled back hard to look up
at the stars it's like when Mama
took us to see that elephant and
it kept getting bigger as we walked
around it like they say in *Good
Housekeeping* you got to put things
in their place get some perspective
remember how winter nearly killed us
then spring hit so sudden like light
in a dark room so much happens quickly
you can't catch gear like my husband
Herman had all his blood go bad such
a big man so scared of his black dreams
I mean we all got our pain my youngest
boy born with no luck his brain twisted
like a turnip but who isn't crippled
life just keeps on happening like
weather he thinks the stars turn on
like television God knows I don't
hate men but maybe it's better alone
a person never knows what's important
why fear is like a door with no handle
and shame hurts so bad when love sours
Kate I said take care of your brother
yes we keep losing people time can be
cruel it's like walking round that big
dark beast hoping it'll add up to something
but it only gets bigger Kate late at night
sometimes I hear death cracking its knuckles

I get so cold not knowing what comes next
then it's another season Kate keep your eyes
on the stars I don't know much but maybe
in your time that beast will stop growing
and you'll blossom into something better
than me Kate you already know it's not easy
being a woman. . . .

Anemone

Once everything was blue
the faces lips blood dreams
the way emotion invades reality
& then things turned green
the floors ladders gardens
opening into fields of such lush
possibility & then the world
turned yellow the hair breath
touch of the woman who pulled him
from one dark wonder into another
& then the stars earth walls sea
he swam night after white night
the drifting through white space
there is no doubt that death
is white the blizzards he feared
would go on forever & then the feast
flaring up like a plague of locusts
yes red is what's left when everything
leaves & time is the last dinner guest
who sits with his legs on the table
toasting the anemone that springs up
like the recrudescence of hope yes
red is the first moment of appetite
opening in the eye like vision

Fifth Avenue in Early Spring

We are admiring Bergdorf's summer fashions,
myself & this young couple who coo & flutter

like cockatoos rife with seasonal pleasure.
The girl dreams aloud about moonlit beaches

while the boy, who obviously adores her,
smiles as if to share the elegance

of her long black hair which lifts like mist
curling off the nearby East River. Yes,

she is lovely, balanced on her toes
like a dancer & I doubt if she

is even thinking about returning
to South Bend or Poughkeepsie

now that we have all survived
another winter in this city

where one earns his papers slowly
& even the satisfactions can be disturbing.

But this is a night when everyone is wistful,
here on a street unlike any other,

where even those of us who are no longer
particularly innocent

are suddenly happy
to bear witness.

Approaching Forty

Suddenly the hours
jam like wreckage
which seems oddly
familiar, if unfocused.
Suddenly the winter
keeps its chill
while spring is fifty
minutes long & summer,
like passion, quickly
loses its perspective.
Suddenly my neighbors
smile in passing & each
day is less a contest
between pleasure &
retribution. Suddenly
the past breaks up
like an iceberg &
my life & I speak
even when we don't
understand each other.
Yes, time has cooled
my fever & if this continues
my guardian angel, Stein,
will soon leave me for
a more complicated man,
but, perhaps, he's done
his job well enough
to last me another
forty years of
embattled celebration.

The Music

There is music in the spheres of the body.
I mean the pull of the sea in the blood
of the man alone on his porch watching
the stars wind bands of light around his body.
I mean the roll of the planet that is the rhythm
of his breath & the wilderness of his perception
that is the immensity of light flowering like stars
in the lights of his eyes. I mean the singing
in his body that is the world of the moment of his life,
Lord!

Lines to a
Jewish Cossack

Lines to a Jewish Cossack:
For Isaac Babel

As a boy I cut his photo from my copy of *Red Cavalry*
& twisted my face to look properly disturbed with vision.
But irony is impossible to imitate & certainly there's
too much amused spirit in his smile though poor output
was the reason he was sent to a writer's camp, which,
let's admit, is a fate fancy enough to end one of his own stories.
Writers aren't often killed for their silence.

Yes, he loved truth too much & politics too little
to be trustworthy in the affairs of state but I think
disappointment is the spice behind the irony in his eyes.
He saw his father on his knees before a mounted Cossack captain
& disgrace is a legacy a son cannot easily forgive.
We have this in common. My father died broken of purse & spirit
& failure is a demeaning debt. I admit my own production isn't
so hot this year—I too fear being sent away.

Once he wrote that a story wasn't finished
until every line he loved most was omitted.
Yes, but the human spirit cannot withstand such revision
& we write to undo the wrong we cannot alter in our lives.

I understand that paradox makes each day
one wink or swallow less absurd & that death,
like self-loathing, can be an engaging companion,
but why would a bespectacled Jewish kid with plump cheeks
& a mind suited to Talmudic study ride with the Philistines
of his age, carrying an unloaded gun into battle—
why husband his own enemies, why such a thing?

On this spring morning it's sweet to imagine us
sipping vodka on the cusp of the Black Sea
like old friends who remain indigenous only
to that pit of ashes we call memory. What if I grew up
on Lake Ontario & am more Baltic in composition—
we share the same ironic disposition as we sit here watching
the good southern light lace our sea with such fine affection,
while swapping stories we must not understand too quickly
lest we lose their mystery, which, like grief & belly-laughter,
must last us at least another century or two.

My Guardian Angel Stein

In our house every floor was a wailing wall
& each sideward glance a history of insult.
Nightly Grandma bolted the doors believing God

had a personal grievance to settle on our heads.
Not Atreus exactly but we had furies (Uncle Jake
banged the tables demanding respect from fate) & enough

outrage to impress Aristotle with the prophetic unity
of our misfortune. No wonder I hid behind the sofa sketching
demons to identify the faces in my dreams & stayed under

bath water until my lungs split like pomegranate seeds.
Stein arrived one New Year's Eve fresh from a salvation in Budapest.
Nothing in his 6,000 years prepared him for our nightly bacchanal

of immigrant indignity except his stint in the Hundred Years' War
where he lost his eyesight & faith both. This myopic angel knew
everything about calamity (he taught King David the art of hubris

& Moses the price of fame) & quoted Dante to prove others
had it worse. On winter nights we memorized the Dead Sea Scrolls
until I could sleep without a night light & he explained why

the stars appear only at night ("Insomniacs, they study the Torah
all day!"). Once I asked him outright: "Stein, why is our house
so unhappy?" Adjusting his rimless glasses, he said: "Boychick,

life is a comedy salted with despair. All humans are disappointed.
Laugh yourself to sleep each night & with luck, pluck & credit cards
you'll beat them at their own game. Catharsis is necessary in this house!"

Ah, Stein, bless your outsized wings & balding pate & while I'm at it
why not bless the imagination's lonely fray with time, which, yes,
like love & family romance, has neither beginning, middle nor end.

In Exile

Dante wrote his wife, Gemma, about his garden
which grew double-breasted roses & plum trees,
but this was in Ravenna, where he lived in exile
for twenty years. It's enough to say he knew something
about Hell, but exile is a strange business & memory
is a kind of Hell & longing, too. Which reminds me
of my uncle Jake who worked in a movie house watching
the same films like one of Dante's sinners replaying
the same crime. Each night he listened to his police radio
in his room off our kitchen & wrote letters to editors
about busted traffic lights & birds starving to death.
When he died I found fifteen shopping bags full of girlie books
& badly rhymed poems about loneliness & unregenerate love.
Dante came out of his room once in a while. He understood
passion & divine punishment & knew there was more to passion
than everlasting fire. Where in his kingdom of the damned
would Jake fit? Jake, who crouched behind his bureau,
rubbing at himself like the sinners Dante placed in a pit,
each damned to gnaw the other's head for eternity. But
their punishment amplified their lives. There's transcendence
in such agony. But there was nothing metaphysical about Jake,
who sat hunched on his perch beside the screen, imprisoned
in his blasphemous fantasy & rage. Ah, Jake, a man who cannot love
is forever exiled from himself. His life is his punishment.
Think of Dante alone in his garden where the starry skies
lit up in realms of fire, music & light. Think of him scribbling
his remorseful visions all night, longing for Florence, for Gemma.
In his every word there is the pain of celebration. Yes, beauty lost
is still splendid in its reinvention. But what about Jake,
whose shoes didn't fit & who cut himself shaving every morning—
Jake, for whom there is no music of the spheres or the forgiveness
of light & who will never again behold the cold passion of the stars.

Interior with Arches: After Piranesi

Look at these stairs leading to barred windows
where pulleys hang heavy as pendulums measuring
centuries of uninterrupted gloom & scaffolding
is fixed forever in stony shadow—silence

has never paid gravity more honor nor has despair
been better fitted to the eye as metaphor, but
I wonder if Piranesi wanted more than desultory
grandeur & if these glum palaces are meant

to warn us against the hundred torments of spring?
What was his fascination for such unhappiness? Was
he joking about our faith in just rewards? Certainly
death's seduction isn't a subject for celebration.

Yes, what have we done that demands such imprisonment,
what is our crime? I think it's best to imagine him
as a comedian of nightmare who doodled his sacred
flèches while flirting with an angel so voluptuous

he had to etch bars in the very air as reminders
of our passion to be punished & the earthly pleasures
we must forsake lest we forget our place which even
angels are too sinful or intelligent to tolerate.

A Letter Found on a January Night in Front of the Public Theater

Dear Emily Pearlmutter,

Today I read how good you are as Nina
and even Chekhov couldn't be so proud
but hearing from me must be a shock
since your grandma said I died from TB
on Ellis Island (if she was alive she'd spit
three times!) but better you should know
the truth and maybe forgive me. I had TB
but my brother Izzy was the one who died.
They wouldn't let him in (imagine after
all our grief being sent back to Russia!)
and after weeks in detention he cut his wrists
on a sardine can (others did the same but used
fancier methods). I'm not making excuses but
life on the Lower East Side was no piknic.
Thousands on each block ate herring and crackers
without a cracked pot to piss in and I wasn't
twenty (and so green my first banana I ate peel
and all and was insulted to eat corn—in Russia
we fed it to pigs!) when grandma had your mother
and day and night we sewed crotches for pennies
the uptown Germans paid (may they eat steak in Hell!).
My cousin Sam broke hands—two bits a knuckle—
and put his own sister on the street (where she didn't
sell pickles!) so maybe it's better not to judge
what you haven't suffered . . .

Your photo in the *Times* shows your grandma's eyes
but I'm afraid you have my mouth that made me
so much trouble always insulting the wrong person.
Like you I was an actor but maybe my most famous role
is wife-deserter. After two years in the Yiddish Theater
I went to Hollywood but with my bad English (a Cambell
soup can I couldn't read without stuttering) got only
extra work and ended up selling plastic legs
after I lost my left one making bombs against Hitler
(one mistook me for a Nazi?). But never I stopped
writting tho your grandma sent back only fishhooks
(not that I blame her—she wiped the blood I coughed
in steerage and fed me her rations eight months pregnant!)
but believe me I've been punished. God put me in this
welfare home for retired actors where each night
lights-out means an encore. When they're not singing Sinatra
they're dancing on my head like Fred Astaire—at least
they keep trying! But failure can be a demanding mistress
and now that you know success early I pray you remember
Nina's lines—"What matters is not fame, not glory . . .
but knowing how to have faith." Talent isn't always
sympathetic so please don't make TV commercials or
hide behind your beauty. Emily, I've written you
maybe a thousand letters but shame isn't postage
and even if you can't forgive me I hope you won't mind
if I'm always in the front row clapping. Be strong
and honest (thank God you didn't change your name!)
and there's nothing you can't accomplish. Darling,
your black hair is so outspoken I break glasses.

> With respectful admiration,
> Lewis Pearlmutter

Ode

Grandma stuffed her fur coat into the icebox.
God Himself couldn't convince her it wasn't a closet.
"God take me away this minute!" was her favorite Friday night prayer.
Nothing made sense, she said. Expect heartburn & bad teeth, not sense.
Leave a meat fork in a dairy dish & she'd break the dish & bury the fork.
"I spit on this house, on this earth & on God for putting me
in this life that spits on me night & day," she cried, forgetting the barley
in barley soup. It wasn't age. She believed she was put here to make
one unforgivable mistake after another. Thou shalt be disappointed
was God's first law. Her last words were: "Turn off the stove
before the house blows up." Listen, I'm thirty-four already
& nothing I do is done well enough. But what if disappointment
is faith & not fate? What if we never wanted anything enough to hurt over?
All I can say is spring came this year with such a wallop
the trees are still shaking. Grandma, what do we want from them?
What do we want?

Personal History

My father is playing solitaire in the last train compartment.
He turns over a card named: The End of the Journey is Grief.
He is after God, the conductor says, taking our unmarked tickets.

My mother stands at the end of the corridor, frozen in her silence
like a fly seized in amber. The train passes the house where I was born
& the wheel in my chest slaps my ribs awake. I wave at myself (the boy

in the attic window) but cannot hear what I am crying as we pass
the cemetery where all our personal history is buried. You will be
remembered only in the dark dreams of strangers, the conductor sings.

Yes, but faith isn't allowed in our century, my mother answers.
We are all born in exile, my father says, turning over a card named:
Diaspora. Yes, it has been that all along, I think, holding my own hand.

My mother anoints me with the brilliant glass of her disaffection
as we all stare out the window into the dark where the stars continue
to survive like syllables of an extinct but beautiful language.

Shane

There was no moon & the horizon a fire breaking
over the black earth & the man on horseback floated
into the red plum of the sky & did not hear the boy
screaming his name & then there was only the earth
& the sky like a clay sea & the boy who believed
it was his imperfection the man was leaving.

My father always slept in movies & we walked home
under the trees & stars without talking & there is
an understanding between fathers & sons & death is
not something a boy can understand & my father was dying
out of his body as I was growing into mine & there was
only the black earth & pale summer sky & the horizon
like a fire breaking on our heads.

The Hemingway House in Key West

If he wrote it he could get rid of it.
—"Fathers and Sons," Ernest Hemingway

My father left me a book of Hemingway's stories
& I understood he meant this as an explanation
& one year later I drove to Idaho to see Hemingway's grave
& phoned his house as if to beg permission for a grief
that held me like a second spine & I saw the room upstairs
where he killed himself & that night I slept dreamless
in a field until the sun's blank stare singed
the loss into my eyes.

Twenty years later I visit Hemingway's house in Key West.
"You look like you want to hear the real dope on Papa,"
the guide says, pointing to the kitchen table raised
to fit Hemingway's height during late-night eating binges.
Like the good wedding guest buttonholed by obsession,
I listen: insomnia, black dreams, his fear of death
without honor—"His father killed himself too,"
the guide sings by rote as we head toward the back cottage
where Hemingway wrote each morning, "depressed, hung over,
he never missed a morning . . . "

I stare at this cottage as if into the pit
his insomniac hunger only deepened.
This was where his despair was hammered
into an alchemy of language that still echoes
in my own insomniac ears. Yes, the sons of failed fathers
have much to undo, but language doesn't soften the pain
that blackens the heart's Torah & absolution
isn't what I am after.

There is something dark in my nature.

One night I woke to see my father staring
out of my bedroom window. "Papa," I cried
as he turned to show me the fire fading
in his eyes like a pilot light. Our shadows
locked like clock hands as he whispered,
"I am bankrupt . . . there's something I must tell you . . . "
but he said nothing & the next morning I found his body
in a bed soaked with urine & his eyes staring at the ceiling
as if asking a last question the silence would never answer.

All my life I have wondered what he meant to tell me.

Jerusalem

Here, under the highest sky
this side of Greenwich Village,

I stand on my hotel terrace,
watching the Old City lights

burn like ancient stars
on Herod's stones, which,

even under such symphonic gloss,
seem embattled. American

to the blood-slap of my bones,
I lift my wine glass high

& salute the pilgrim moon
as it wanders in its dark wilderness.

After all, it too is just
another innocent, stunned,

for a moment, by antiquity
during its long journey home.

Deep Within
the Ravine

Is it possible to explode from within?
—KRISHNAMURTI

1 "Deep Within the Ravine"

All winter he returns to the white room
in the Metropolitan Museum of Art, drawn
by Hans Hofmann's big red square of fire
centered in white viscera like the sun's
cement block bursting into cataracts of
color, here, he thinks, is light's source,
the mind's egg spilling its surplus of obsession
like an infection poisoning the blood, yes,
this painting is the mind devouring itself,
its blue vortex spreading like finger smears
in a child's nightmare, but pain, he thinks,
is perception, a coalescing of color, while
inside the pain is knowledge, a hunger
without boundaries.

All winter he stands wrapped within himself,
deep in the conflux of expanding color that
holds him in his body like a frame, yes,
he thinks, pain is existence & he is bounded
in light, stuck deep within pain's ravine,
his mind is infected.

2 The Rounds Continue;
Christmas 1980

Business is good but Fifth Avenue
mocks his indigence with gold ashtrays
from Bulgaria; mere details in some final
accounting, say, a bullish apocalypse
where hope is bought on credit & death
is just another sad cliché wrapped in tinsel.
Like the salesboy in FAO Schwarz's window
who clips the gossamer wings of a toy angel,
obsessed with self-expression. But the season
demands such crippling of spirit as each day's
headlines offer despair as solace: in Harlem
a woman shoots her nephew for complaining
about his breakfast, while, downtown,
a professor's wife walks her infant son
out of her tenth-floor window. His woman
left him too & he feels dropped from ten floors up.
Why does the mind destroy what it loves most,
why must we crush our last hope of continuance?
he wonders, roaming the streets like a blind man
after inner vision as Stein, his guardian angel,
overweight & unaccustomed to such devout self-loathing,
hurries to keep pace. "You need a woman full-grown
of heart and mind, that's remedy for self-mythification.
Meantime, let's see a movie or have an ice cream."
But he is stuck in the ruins of the year's last cruel intake
of breath. He cannot eat or sleep; abandoned & betrayed,
his rounds continue. Today, he reads, a white man
is slashing blacks for crowding up the Lower East Side
& he imagines the souls of the professor's wife & infant
flying over Madison Avenue in a last effort at transcendence.

3 The Dead Sea of Memory

Sunday mornings are best (before
minimizers bring art news: "Hofmann's
last wife was young so he was in a hurry
but mostly he was a teacher anyway.") but
Tuesdays & Thursdays are worse after his shrink
questions his obsession (Stein prefers his own
methods & sits in the waiting room reading Spinoza)
& now his foot hurts for no reason & he limps
from color to color while Stein protests: "I'm no critic
but how about something more figurative, like Rubens'
juicy nudes, even Chagall would be refreshing after
so much crazy abstraction."

Deep in the red square center his father smiles
from inside a red Cadillac & he remembers the auto show
where girls in swimsuits played John Philip Sousa
on banjoes as his father turned & turned under colored lights
& how, years later, he drove his father's old Ford wagon
back from his funeral as rain hammered the rusted metal
& the streets & sky & light were bankrupt of color
& now he rides subways with Stein who won't shut up.
"Kid, you took a different road, but failure isn't legacy,
enjoy that ghetto blaster, in Manhattan subways are faster
than Cadillacs." Yes, it is his luck to end up zigzagging
this glutted island with only the Dead Sea of his memory
& a verbose ionized angel for company.

4 "Profound Longing"

This Sunday a woman steps up & smiles.
She is tall & her black hair is fastened
by an ivory heart-shaped pin. "Everything
he knew went into this painting," she says,
"but what does 'Deep Within the Ravine' mean?"
He thinks: *You*. But he is stuck & cannot speak.
The professor's wife carries her infant deep
into his mind's ravine. What's wrong? her eyes ask.
Yes, he thinks, this silence is unnatural, but his foot
aches & his tongue turns to salt. She shrugs & moves on
to Hofmann's "Profound Longing" where she smiles at
another man who responds with conversation. Yes,
it's that simple, he thinks, ignoring Stein who
curses him in ten languages. This infection
will end him yet, he thinks, limping off across
the floor's loud echoing membrane.

5　The Red Square Center

Beveled of mind, he sits in the gloom
of a girlie show while Stein squirms
with shame. "This dump won't help, but
stay if you must, I'll wait outside."
Two months' rent behind, his foot keeps
him home from work & today his woman wrote:
"Sure I miss you but your pain swallows me.
My shrink says I need a man who makes money
and dry-cleans his sweaters regularly." Yes,
his pain breaks him into a hall of mirrors
where he cannot bear his own scrutiny.
Against the screen's violent emporium
he replays humiliation's every detail:
Marsha of the country club who called him
her "Peasant Jew stud from town" & joked
about his father's epic failures as if
disgrace was a claim to celebrity. When
he showed her his hill above the reservoir,
where he hid spring mornings in lilac-scented
elms, she said, "We got bigger hills at the club."
"Get out of here!" Stein cries from the balcony.
"Remember, Hofmann pushed his vision beyond
pain's indulgence. There are other women, pal."
But he's stuck in fantasy, deep in his red
square center, focus of the heart's uproar.
Three rows back, his father snores, dreaming,
he imagines, about red Cadillacs. Still,
he recalls how light scraped the reservoir's
cement wings high on that roll of hill where
time itself stilled in praise of early longing.
Stein's right, he thinks, dumps like this won't help.

6 The Odds Increase; New Year's Eve

Call it modern concupiscence or variegated culture
but tonight even God won't step into a doorway
unannounced. Greenwich Village is six corners
& a subway island where jugglers, fire-swallowers
& outlaw thespians compete with winos singing Verdi
to the dumbstruck stars; each bar classifies: Gay,
Straight & Presbyterian as he limps toward his Sunday *Times*
& two fat cigars through the juggernaut of horns & confetti.
Yes, once again, the New Year; but fear is the spine holding
him upright. His mind insists someone is always not on his side
as each hour the odds increase against sanity; he's lost his job
& his landlord has nailed a warning to his door & now he's side-
swept by a black boy in red hotpants who skates by with headphones
pinned like glowworms to his bobbing head. In front of Village Cigars
(owned by five Jewish black belts from Queens) the Lady of Salvation
thumps her bible at a transvestite who harangues a blue pompadour,
camping for the limousines that cruise two blond youths who think
7th Avenue is a runway for pubescent charm. Yet tourists eye him
as if he's the oddball which he is: shoes shined, tie & collared,
his eyes scouting the opposing sex, he stands out, a freak
of circumstance, come to witness the West's sad decline,
eh, Stein?

7 The Next Ice Age

His stalagmite posture isn't camouflage
as he sits in the museum cafeteria with
his bad foot hoisted on a chair & Stein
miming his constant wincing ("What're you
ducking—God's wrath?") & now not even
Hofmann offers succor as he tosses pennies
into the goldfish pond for: Faith, Love &
Obeisance to Art, while, across the far
marble shore a small girl watches as if he's
a statue sprung to life, which isn't far off,
he thinks, feeling like an exhibit of mutant
imperfection. He smiles & she hides her eyes,
feigning feminine alarm, but her toothless smile
is a token, he thinks, of regeneration's healing
custom so he plugs his ears & wags his tongue
as Stein whispers, "Easy, boychick, I've a report
to file!" Hands on hips, the child contemplates
her options, then ups the stakes: hopping one-
legged like a wounded rabbit. Not to be outdone,
he holds his bad foot & leaps into the air as Stein,
who believes he's seen everything, hollers: "Even
Samson knew restraint! Job wasn't this pathetic!"
Hah! Stein is paranoid as the Old Testament, he smiles,
performing three deep knee bends. *Beat that,* kid!
Tugging at her pigtail, she squints, then suddenly
her ostrich white undies glisten in the fluorescent air
as she stands on her hands, smiling at him upside down!
"Okay," Stein says, "but I hope you split your skull!"
His legs lift high above his head as applause erupts

& yes, the world looks better upside down. But now
the girl's mother has returned with food & the girl
is caught mid-flight in a cartwheel. Dragged away kicking,
she stops to curtsy at the door. "So long, Lambchop!"
he calls, brushing himself off. Yes, Mama, he thinks,
instruct your seedling not to play with strangers,
though this one's harmless enough, he's just biding
his time toward the next ice age which, with luck,
will galvanize all his vain posturing into another
brackish relic of his all too quickly passing kind.

8 Pain's Spider Web

Fly in the ointment, he's stuck
in pain's spider web, midway up
the museum stairs, his foot is fat
with rage as endless marble waves
rock him deeper into his mind's
mud hut while people rush toward
evidence of civilization's glory,
unaware, he thinks, of the swamp
he's drowning in, that pit they all
sprung from like bits of prehistoric
light blinking in the blackest night.
One woman stops to take his hand & sobs
split his chest but she hurries on
as Stein waits on the bottom step,
too weary to try even a wing at rescue.
Yes, his mind is overwhelmed with light,
he cannot move up or down & his spine
spins with pain's electric current while
speakers count the moments left until
closing time.

9 Infection

It begins in his big toe
& soon his whole foot
is redolent as spiny lobster,
so he bathes it in ice, raises
it on pillows where long red lines
break up his leg like tributaries
of masculine vainglory. "For shame!"
cries Stein, "you're back-stroking
up the Styx and I'm not Cerberus
even if you think I own three tongues!"
But now his crotch is inflamed & he slips
into his fever's warm surf & wakes to Stein
pacing his hospital bed, a needle stuck deep
in his wrist. "It's time we faced the truth.
This is nothing less than self-castration!"
At night a nurse measures his life's tide
& deep in his red square center she carries
him into a cataract of light where his mind's
egg bursts into flames of pure color. Yes,
he thinks, this fever is the mind's manifest
destiny & he's unfurling back to his source
in a torrent of damaged cells. "Well, I see
you're still among the living," the nurse smiles,
nodding at his erection. Watch out, he thinks,
this infection is a lizard's tongue that means
to pour its venom down both our throats until
our bodies dance with rage, until, like blood grapes,
we explode from our centers, Lord!

10 The Fronts

When the gods afflict us, we are obliged
to bear our misfortunes; but must people pity
a man who suffers through his own choice?
                    —Edmund Wilson

Hidden away inside his mind's hard shrubbery,
he reads about Philoctetes, whose leg betrayed him, too.
"String your bow," Stein says, fluffing his pillow.
"Philoctetes was finally rescued. This is just another
white room." Yes, but he's drunk on gallons of penicillin,
his mind is hairy as heliotrope—he cannot stop talking
to himself in third person! "The mind prepares its own
ordeals," says Stein, limping in mock sympathy. "First
the collapse, then the rebuilding. See it as a test of spirit!"
Yes, but one front is always breaking: money, love & work—
he stretches himself too thin & falls short. He's sick of it all!
"Disappointment is the tax from womb to grave," Stein sighs,
"fate isn't glacial drift but a tapestry dense with details
of the soul's apocalypse. Hold back & wait!" Tossing in bed
like a beast after an itch that refuses all satisfaction,
he's deaf to Stein's homilies; inside each moment's ingot
he swallows himself whole. He's lonely for his own kind!
Stein smiles. "Friend, there's always too much of everything
—your only infection is life."

11 Mysterious Kitchens

Channel the congresses, nightly sessions . . .
Mysterious kitchens. . . . You shall search them all.
                                        —*Hart Crane*

Winter's end & his appetite returns,
unraveling its onionskin of instinct,
yes, enslaved again to that sorry master,
sexual desire, he continues his far-flung
nightly flights, pressed against a stranger's
backside, the woman straphanging beside him
avoids his eyes as they sway hip to thigh, ah
this libidinous town, he cannot recall what
he wanted from such rapturous disturbance,
indulgences of the most wretched city kind,
immigrant expectation embedded in the eyes
of grocery clerks & subway sweepers like
an engendering foliage of pain, this is
the prize after such furious overreaching,
his father desired glory after his long traffic
from Russian peasantry, performing Rockefeller
imitations with his good woman & odd-minded son
clapping, pointed here by fate's compass needle
& his faith in regeneration, he died bankrupt
of all passion & now his son stands snapping
to the hot punk rock on 3rd Avenue, he & his
undaunted angel at large in nighttime Hades,
amid the ragged symmetry of bronze gardens
blazing like ruins in his mind's annealing furnace,
under this high pearly parallax of stars burning
like refugees hungry for a glimpse of the Promised Land,
oh what comedy-charade, macadam springing up like Hofmann's
fiery verdigris from Central Park to Hoboken, yes, so many
high-tuned limbs sashaying in nylon & hot polish, so many
mysterious kitchens to discover deep in the squandering
of his 36th year, crippled, forlorn & guilty, he has arrived,
the singing residue of all his haphazard wanderings, here
he stands, upright almost—a citizen of the big town!

12 The Spectacle of the Rest of Our Lives

Here in this city island where faith
is a nightly journey through the mind's
isolated republics & God is mere nostalgia
for a rectitude that splits the soul into
hemispheres of fire & ice, here, where stars
drift like refugees gathering to witness
their generation's deliquescence & despair's
cruel disorders explode into nightmares of
sexual pyrotechnics, here, where sewers exhale
Satan's wrath & all-night bars purge the bankrupt
with visions of a besotted paradise, here,
where nothing changes while nothing stays the same
& redemption is forever an inch out of reach—
the benumbed century hurries toward its Armageddon
like a badly spliced newsreel in which the clipped wings
of a toy angel hanging in one of a million tinseled windows
spins in his eye's drugged prism as just another detail
in the ongoing story which is known among humans & angels alike
as the spectacle of the rest of our lives.

The Quality

The Quality

There is in each body something splendid, I think,
　　　a kind of sheltering, say, the suit of
hours we wear like weather, or instinct striking
　　　the spine's cold accordion, that ripening
of reflex that is the mind's appetite for testimony,
　　　yes, in darkness there is strength hoarded

against damage, say, the flowering of desire imprinted
　　　in the infant's smile as it awakens out of
its dream of creation, I mean pain is not sentiment only,
　　　but a fierce healing, like light rebuilding,
out of darkness, our original boundaries, yet something
　　　is lost in the growing, yes, the greater

the gift the more troubling the sleep, like lovers lost
　　　in the body's cold spin, we are naked
within the shell of our temperament, beings greater in
　　　mystery after violation, yes, like strips
of horizon, the spirit unwinds its gift of a single life,
　　　moment by moment, say, that quality of love

that is not physical, but sensed, like vision burning
　　　in the eye's garden, yes, once again spring
arrives after winter's long ash & I accept despair's
　　　selfish fruit as the fermenting of wonder
that springs out of everything lost & dying, say,
　　　that furthering of instinct, which, like

the spider's ambition to infinitely extend its life
　　　another inch of light, glistens like rain
over the attic window where I sat as a boy entranced
　　　with the radiance of first longing, yes,
a quality so distinctly human we glow like light burning
　　　over all the fire-struck windows of our lives.

Grateful acknowledgment is made to the following for permission to reprint copyrighted material:

Chatto & Windus, the Translator's Literary Estate, and A. P. Watt Ltd.: A selection from "The Seagull" from *Tales and Plays* by Anton Tchekov, translated by Constance Garnett.

Farrar, Straus and Giroux, Inc.: An excerpt from *The Wound and The Bow* by Edmund Wilson. Copyright 1929, 1932, 1940, 1941 by Edmund Wilson. Copyright renewed © 1966, 1968, 1970 by Edmund Wilson.

Liveright Publishing Corporation: Lines from "The Tunnel" from *The Bridge* are reprinted from *The Complete Poems and Selected Letters and Prose of Hart Crane,* edited by Brom Weber. Copyright 1933, © 1958, 1966 by Liveright Publishing Corporation.

Penguin Books Ltd: An excerpt from *The Poems of Catullus,* translated and with an introduction by Peter Whigham (A Penguin Classic). This translation and Introduction copyright © 1966 by Peter Whigham.

Charles Scribner's Sons and Jonathan Cape Limited, on behalf of the Executors of the Ernest Hemingway Estate: The quotation from "Fathers and Sons" in *Winner Take Nothing.* Copyright 1933 by Charles Scribner's Sons; copyright renewed 1961 by Mary Hemingway.